King Solomon's Mines

SIR H. RIDER HAGGARD

Level 4

Retold by David Maule

Series Editors: Andy Hopkins and Jocelyn Potter

Pearson Education Limited
Edinburgh Gate, Harlow,
Essex CM20 2JE, England
and Associated Companies throughout the world.

ISBN: 978-1-4058-6513-5

First published by Penguin Books 2000
This edition published 2008

19

Illustrations by Mark Peppé

Typeset by Graphicraft Ltd, Hong Kong
Set in 11/14pt Bembo
Printed in Great Britain
SWTC/07

Published by Pearson Education Ltd

Contents

Introduction

We crept inside the cave, and sat close together. We could not sleep; the cold was too terrible.

At last the air began to grow grey with light. The sun looked in on our half-frozen bodies – and also on Ventvogel, who was sitting there dead among us.

Shocked, we stood up and moved away from his dead body. Then I heard a cry of fear from somebody, and turned my head. Sitting at the end of the cave, there was another body. The head rested on its chest, and the long arms hung down. I stared at it. It too was a dead man – and a white man. The body was completely frozen.

We are in a freezing mountain cave in Africa in the early 1880s. Allan Quatermain, an English adventurer and hunter, is helping Sir Henry Curtis and his friend, Captain Good, to find Sir Henry's missing brother, Neville. Neville disappeared while he was travelling north into the heart of Africa, looking for the famous but undiscovered King Solomon's Mines. Quatermain has a rough map of the way to the mines. It was drawn by José da Silvestra, a Portuguese adventurer from the 1500s, who had died trying to find the treasure. Quatermain agrees to help Sir Henry in return for part of the treasure, or money for his son if he is killed on the journey. He does not have much hope that they will return alive. As they travel north towards the desert and the mountains, a mysterious young Zulu man, Umbopa, asks to join them on their journey. They cross the desert, almost dying of thirst, and climb to the top of a mountain, where they find a cave. After a freezing night, they wake up and discover that Ventvogel, one of their African helpers, has frozen to death. And there is another dried, frozen body...

Who is the dead man inside the cave? Will Sir Henry find his missing brother? Will the adventurers find the treasure of King Solomon's Mines? Do the mines even exist? Who is Umbopa, and why does he want to join the three Englishmen on their mad, dangerous journey?

Before we find the answers to these questions, we must join the four adventurers as they cross the mountains into the green, unmapped forests of Kukuanaland. We will meet many strange people: the murderous King Twala, a frightening old witch called Gagool (who says that she is hundreds of years old!) and the beautiful Foulata. We will share unforgettable experiences with the adventurers, both good and bad: we will witness cruel murders, be tricked by dangerous enemies, suffer the sadness of an impossible love and fight in a terrible battle. But we will also enjoy the excitement of looking for hidden treasure.

Will it be found? Read *King Solomon's Mines*, one of the most famous and exciting adventure stories in English literature, and find out!

Allan Quatermain has many qualities that British people of the late 1800s admired, but the real hero of the book is Sir Henry Curtis. He is a true gentleman, and a better fighting man than Quatermain. Haggard, the real writer of this story, admired these qualities; strangely, he did not really admire writers. When Sir Henry asks Quatermain to help him, Quatermain (as we have already seen) does the job for money. He cannot afford to be a true gentleman.

While the real men of that time were outside, killing and dying, weaker men spent their time in the company of women. Rider Haggard did marry, but he was always rather shy with women. This may explain why there are only two female characters in the book – and one of them is Gagool, a horrible old witch. The other, an African woman called Foulata, falls in love with Captain Good. Good is less of a hero than Curtis or even Quatermain, and he also falls in love with her. A mixed-race relationship would, though, be shocking to the outside world.

Haggard's view of African characters and society can be difficult for modern readers. He was a man of his time and so Africans were not equal to Europeans, but one experience did change his ideas a little. In January 1879, Haggard was in Pretoria when news arrived that the Zulus had destroyed a British army of 1,600 men at Isandhlwana. This was a great shock and, although the British won the war, they admired the fighting qualities of the Zulus. Haggard's good opinion of these people is shown in the character of Umbopa, the Zulu who joins the three white men on their search.

It is still a fact, though, that the people of the lost country of Kukuanaland in this book seem rather childlike. They are greatly affected by simple things like Captain Good's false teeth and eyeglass, and they do not understand what an eclipse is. But in Rider Haggard's defence, he knew his subject better than most men, and his ideas are more modern that many of his time.

When Haggard was in Africa, the old city of Zimbabwe had recently been discovered. He did not visit the area but he certainly read about it. Many people did not believe that Zimbabwe, with its high stone walls, had been built by Africans. They believed that it was part of the old land of Sheba, home of the Queen of Sheba, who brought presents of gold and valuable stones to King Solomon in Jerusalem. Today we think that Sheba was in Yemen, and that Zimbabwe was built by local people between the years 1250 and 1450, a very long time after the death of Solomon.

It is difficult to believe that there could be any contact between southern Africa and Jerusalem. Haggard makes this easier by reducing the distance between them. He places Kukuanaland a long way to the north of Zimbabwe, in today's southern Zaire. When Quatermain and his friends arrive there, they have travelled a third of the way to Cairo, the capital city of Egypt. They are also only three months' walk from the old port areas of Dar es Salaam and Zanzibar, along routes that were old before Solomon was born. Gold has crossed from Ghana to the Middle East as far back into history as we know. Nobody can be sure that diamonds did not travel from southern Africa.

At the time when *King Solomon's Mines* was written, most Europeans in Africa lived quite near the coast and nobody knew much about the rest of the continent. Rider Haggard's readers could accept that this story was real. This was his greatest skill.

The story is as popular now as it was when it was first written. Many films have been made of it. Perhaps the best one was made in 1950, with Stewart Granger as Quatermain. Of course, films usually change the story of the book in many important ways. Films of *King Solomon's Mine*s always include a young, attractive female adventurer for Quatermain to fall in love with! In 1950, the female character was played by Deborah Kerr. Later, in a 1985 film, it was Sharon Stone.

H. Rider Haggard was born on 22 June 1856 in Norfolk, England. He was the eighth of ten children; his father was in the legal profession and his mother wrote poems. Haggard was not a successful student. Instead of going to university, he was sent by his father to work as a secretary to the governor of Natal in South Africa. His experiences in southern Africa during the war between the English and the Zulus and the first war between the English and the Dutch gave him important material for his future fictional writing.

In 1880, Haggard married Mariana Margitson. (Later, he named three of his daughters after female characters in his books.) In 1881, Haggard returned to England and, like his father, worked in the law, but he was more interested in writing. *King Solomon's Mines* (1885) was his fourth book, and it was written as a result of the success of Robert Louis Stevenson's *Treasure Island*, which came out in the same year. Haggard was asked playfully by one of his brothers to write a better story. Haggard accepted the invitation, and wrote *King Solomon's Mines* in six weeks. When the book came out in September 1885, large advertisements all over London said that it was 'The Most Wonderful Book Ever Written'. It became an immediate best-seller. Haggard almost sold his story for just 500 dollars, but he decided at the last minute on 10% of the future sales. The book made him a rich man.

King Solomon's Mines is important for a number of reasons. It was the first fictional story in English about adventure in Africa, which was in those days still a largely undiscovered continent. Unlike other Victorian writers like Dickens, Trollope and Wilkie Collins, Haggard decided to tell the story from the point of view of one of its characters. Many other writers followed his example. *King Solomon's Mines* also started a fashion for stories about 'Lost Worlds'. Rudyard Kipling's *The Man Who Would Be King* (1888), Edgar Rice Burroughs's *Tarzan* stories (from 1912), Arthur Conan Doyle's *The Lost World* (1912) and Edgar Wallace's *King Kong* (1932) are just a few famous examples.

After the success of *King Solomon's Mines*, Haggard wrote more than fifty books, including many with Allan Quatermain as the main character. His 1887 story *She* is still well-known today, but the others are largely forgotten. *King Solomon's Mines*, though, continues to excite and entertain readers all round the world.

H. Rider Haggard died in London on 14 May 1925. One of his daughters, L.R. Haggard, wrote a book about her memories of her father, *The Cloak That I Left*, in 1951.

Chapter 1 I Meet Sir Henry Curtis

It is a strange thing that at the age of fifty-five I am trying to write a history. I wonder what sort of history it will be! I have done many things in my life, which seems a long one because I started so young. At an age when other boys are at school, I was working here in Africa. I have been buying and selling, hunting, fighting or mining since then, but I only started making real money eight months ago. It is a lot of money, but I do not think I would experience the last fifteen or sixteen months again for it. I am not a brave man, I do not like violence, and I am tired of adventure.

I am not a writer either. I am only writing this for two good reasons: Sir Henry Curtis and Captain John Good asked me to do it; and it may entertain my son Harry, who is studying to be a doctor over there in Liverpool.

It is now about eighteen months since I first met Sir Henry Curtis and Captain Good. Before that I was elephant hunting beyond Bamangwato, and I had had bad luck. Everything went wrong on that trip, and then I got a bad fever too. When I was well enough, I travelled down to the Diamond Fields, sold everything, paid my hunters and moved on to the Cape. After a week there, I decided to go back to Durban by ship. So I joined the *Dunkeld*, which was waiting for passengers from England on another ship. When they arrived, we went to sea.

Two of the new passengers, who seemed to be friends, interested me. One was a man of about thirty, and was one of the largest and strongest-looking men I ever saw. He had yellow hair, a big yellow beard and large grey eyes. I never saw a finer looking man. His face was also familiar, but I could not think why. I learned later that his name was Sir Henry Curtis.

The other man, Sir Henry's friend, was short, rather fat, and dark. He was very tidy, and he always wore an eyeglass in his right eye. It seemed to grow there; it had no string, and he never took it out in daylight except to clean it. At first I thought he used to sleep in it, but I was wrong. He put it in his pocket, with his very fine false teeth, when he went to bed. His name, I discovered from the passenger list, was Good – Captain John Good.

On the first evening there was a high wind. It became very cold and I stood near the engines where it was warm. Captain Good was already there, perhaps for the same reason. We started a conversation and then we joined Sir Henry Curtis at his table for dinner. The captain and I soon started talking about shooting, and I think we discussed most of the animals in Africa. Some time after coffee had been served, he began to ask about elephants.

'Ah, sir,' called somebody behind me, 'you are sitting with the right man. Hunter Quatermain will be able to tell you about elephants if any man can.'

Sir Henry Curtis, who had sat quietly listening to our talk, looked surprised. He bent forward and said in a deep voice, 'Excuse me, sir, but is your name Allan Quatermain?'

I said it was.

Sir Henry smiled suddenly, and Good also looked pleased. 'This is very fortunate,' said Sir Henry, then continued: 'Mr Quatermain, the year before last, I believe you were at a place called Bamangwato, to the north of the Transvaal.'

'I was,' I agreed.

'Did you meet a man called Neville there?'

'Oh, yes. He stopped for a few weeks to rest his cattle. I received a letter about him a few months ago. I answered it as well as I could at the time.'

'Yes,' said Sir Henry, 'I saw your letter. In it you said that Neville left Bamangwato at the beginning of May. He was in a

Sir Henry smiled suddenly, and Good also looked pleased.

wagon with a driver, and a hunter called Jim, and planned to go to Inyati. There he hoped to sell his wagon and continue on foot. You also said that he did sell his wagon, because six months later you saw another man with it. He told you that he had bought the wagon at Inyati from a white man, and that the white man, with one servant, had gone on a shooting trip.'

'Yes.'

There was a pause. 'Mr Quatermain,' Sir Henry said suddenly, 'do you know anything else about the reason for my – for Neville's journey?'

'I have heard something,' I answered, and stopped.

Sir Henry and Captain Good looked at each other, and Captain Good said, 'Tell him.'

'Mr Quatermain,' said Sir Henry, 'I am going to tell you a story, and to ask for your advice, and perhaps for your help. After I got your letter, I asked people about you. They said that you were a good man, and could keep a secret.'

I did not know what to say, so I drank some more coffee.

'Mr Neville was my brother,' Sir Henry continued.

'Oh,' I said. That was why Sir Henry's face looked familiar to me. His brother was a much smaller man and had a dark beard, but his eyes were the same grey colour and his face was in many ways the same.

'He was,' Sir Henry told me, 'my only brother, and we were very close – until something happened about five years ago, and we argued. I was angry, and I behaved badly.'

Captain Good showed that he agreed.

'At about the same time,' Sir Henry continued, 'our father died. He had not written anything down, so all his property and money came to me, the eldest son. My brother did not get a penny, and I offered him nothing. I waited for him to come to me, but he did not come. I am sorry to have to tell you all of this, Mr Quatermain, but I must make things clear.'

'I am sure,' said Captain Good, 'that Mr Quatermain will keep your story to himself.'

'Of course,' I said.

'Well,' Sir Henry said, 'my brother had some money in the bank. He took it out, changed his name to Neville, and came to South Africa. He hoped to make money here. Three years passed and I heard nothing of him, though I wrote several times. I became more and more anxious about him and tried to discover where he was. That is why the letter came to you, and I got your reply. In the end, I decided to come out here and look for him myself, and Captain Good kindly came with me.'

'Yes,' said the captain. 'I have nothing else to do, you see. They say I am too old for the sea. And now perhaps, Mr Quatermain, you will tell us what you know about the gentleman called Neville.'

Chapter 2 The Story of Solomon's Mines

'I have never told this to another person until today,' I answered. 'I heard that he was looking for Solomon's mines.'

'Solomon's mines!' cried both my hearers. 'Where are they?'

'I do not know,' I said. 'I know where people say they are. Once I saw the mountains that defend them. But there were 125 miles of desert between me and them, and I only know one white man who ever got across it. Perhaps I should tell you the story of Solomon's mines as I know it. But you must promise not to say anything to anybody without my permission. Do you agree to that?'

Both of them agreed.

'It was about thirty years ago,' I said. 'I was on my first elephant hunt in the Matabele country. I met a man called Evans – and the poor fellow was killed the next year by an elephant. But one night we were talking about the history of the country, and Evans said, "Did you ever hear of the Suliman Mountains, to the north-west of the Mashukulumbwe country?" I told him I never had. "Ah, well," he said, "that is where King Solomon had his diamond mines. An old witch-doctor up in the Manica country told me all about it. She said that the people on the other side of those mountains were related to the Zulus, and spoke a language like the Zulu language. She said that powerful witches lived among them, and these witches had the secret of a wonderful mine of 'bright stones'."

'I laughed at the story at the time. But twenty years later, I learned something more about the Suliman Mountains and the country beyond them. I was at a place called Sitanda's Kraal when a Portuguese man arrived. He told me that his name was José Silvestre. I was able to help him in a few ways. When he left, he said, "Goodbye. If we ever meet again, I will be the richest man in the world."

'Two weeks later, he came back from the desert. He was carried into my camp by two of my hunters. His lips were dry, and his tongue was black. I did everything I could, but he was dying. When he was able to speak, he said, in a very faint voice, "Listen, friend. I am dying, I know. You have been good to me, so I will give you the writing. Perhaps you will get there if you can cross the desert."

'He felt inside his shirt and brought out a piece of yellow cloth. Something was written on it in red-brown letters. With the cloth were a piece of paper and a map.

'His voice was growing weaker as he said, "The paper shows what is written on the cloth. It took me years to read it. My relative, José da Silvestra, wrote it 300 years ago when he was dying on those mountains. His servant brought the writing back. It has been in the family since then."

'José Silvestre died soon after that. I have had the writing translated into English. Here is a copy.'

> I am José da Silvestra. I am dying of hunger in a little cave on the north side of one of the mountains which I have called Sheba's Breasts. The cave is in the south of the two mountains. I am writing this in the year 1590 with my own blood. My pen is a piece of bone, my paper is a piece of cloth from my shirt. If my servant finds this when he comes, he will bring it to Delagoa, to my friend ... [The name is not clear.] My friend should tell the king my story, and the king should send an army. If the army can cross the desert, fight against the Kukuana people and win, he will become the richest king on earth. I have seen with my own eyes millions of diamonds. They are kept in Solomon's Treasure Room behind the White Death. But Gagool, the witch, cheated me, and I brought nothing away. I was lucky to escape with my life. Whoever comes must follow the map and climb the snow of Sheba's left breast until he reaches the top. On the far side is the great road that Solomon made. From there it is three days' journey to the king's palace. He must kill Gagool.
>
> José da Silvestra

When I had finished reading, and shown them a copy of the map, there was a long silence.

'Well,' said Captain Good, 'I have been round the world twice, and visited most ports, and I have never heard such a strange story.'

'It *is* very strange, Mr Quatermain,' said Sir Henry. 'You are not having a joke with us, strangers in this country?'

'If you think that, Sir Henry,' I said, putting the paper and the map back in my pocket, 'then that is the end of it.' I stood to go.

Sir Henry also stood up and put a large hand on my shoulder. 'Please sit down, Mr Quatermain,' he said. 'I am sorry I doubted you.'

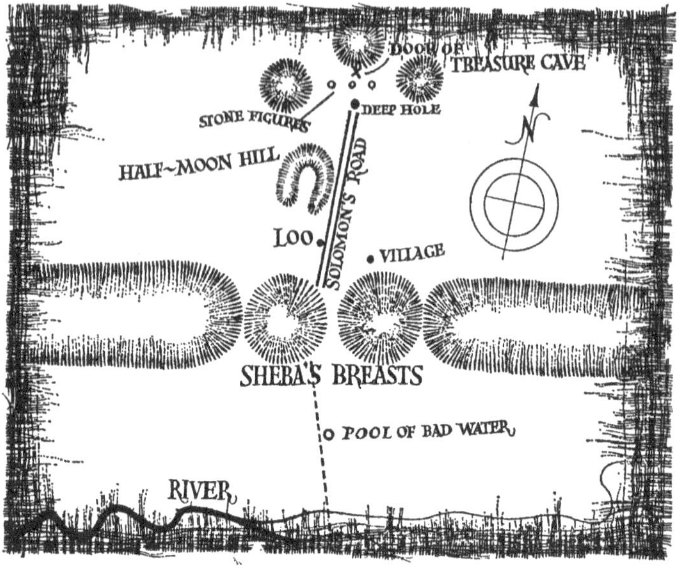

Whoever comes must follow the map . . .

'You can see the real map and writing when we reach Durban,' I said, feeling a little better. 'But I have not told you about your brother. I knew the man Jim, who was with him. He was a Bechuana, a good hunter and a very clever man. He told me that they were going to look for diamonds in the Suliman Mountains. I said that they would die if they did, and now I am afraid . . .'

'Mr Quatermain,' said Sir Henry, 'I am going to look for my brother. I am going to follow him to Suliman's Mountains, and over them if necessary. I will find him, or discover that he is dead. Will you come with me?'

I am not, as I have said, a brave man, and I did not like the idea. The journey meant certain death. Also, I had a son and I needed to continue sending him money. I could not afford to die.

'No, thank you, Sir Henry, I do not think so,' I answered. 'I am too old for this sort of thing, and we would only finish like my poor friend Silvestre. I have a son, and I have to stay alive for him.'

'Mr Quatermain,' said Sir Henry, 'I am a rich man, and I want to go on this journey. I will pay you a generous amount of money before we start. If anything happens to you, your son will receive enough money to finish his studies. And if we reach this place, and find diamonds, they will belong to you and Good. I do not want them. And, of course, I shall pay all the costs of the journey.'

'Sir Henry,' I said, 'this is the best offer that I have ever had. But the job is the biggest that I have ever heard of. I will give you my answer when we get to Durban.'

'Very good,' answered Sir Henry, and then I said good night and went to bed. I dreamed about poor Silvestre and the diamonds.

Chapter 3 Umbopa

I thought about Sir Henry Curtis's offer for a day or two. We did not discuss it, although we talked a lot about hunting. We met again on the night we arrived in Durban. They asked me what I had decided.

'Yes, gentlemen,' I said, 'I will go with you. I have worked here in Africa for many years, and I have never made much money. Most elephant hunters do not live for more than four or five years. I have already lived much longer, but sooner or later I will be killed. Then there will be very little for my son. So I will go with you – but . . .'

'Tell me,' said Sir Henry.

'You will pay all my costs,' I said, 'and Captain Good and I will share the diamonds if we find them. You will pay me £500 for my work on this trip, before we start. You will agree, in writing, that if I die or am badly hurt, you will pay my boy Harry £200 a year for five years.'

'I am very happy to agree,' said Sir Henry.

When we left the ship, Sir Henry and Captain Good stayed at my house. I then bought a wagon and some Zulu cattle to pull it. We packed enough food for the journey, and other things that we would need. Good, who had some medical knowledge, added a box of medicine. We also took three heavy elephant guns, six rifles and three revolvers. Sir Henry had brought some of these from England and some were mine.

We decided that we would need a driver, a leader, and three other men. They had to be good workers and brave men. I found the driver and the leader, and at last we agreed on two others – Ventvogel, an excellent hunter, and Khiva, a young Zulu with some knowledge of English. I looked for a fifth man, but without success.

The evening before we left, Khiva told me that a Zulu named Umbopa wanted to see me. A tall, fine-looking man entered, about thirty years old. He sat on the floor in the corner and stayed silent. His face looked familiar. Then I remembered. I had talked to this man, who commanded some of our African soldiers, on the day before the battle of the Little Hand in that unfortunate Zulu War. He told me, a guide, that he thought the camp was in danger. Afterwards I thought of his words.

'I remember you,' I said. 'What do you want?'

'I hear that you are going on a journey far into the north with the white chiefs from over the water. Is it true?'

'It is.'

'I would like to travel with you. I want no money, but I am a brave man and I can earn my place and meat.'

This man seemed different from other Zulus. I was also not happy about his offer to come without pay. I asked Sir Henry and Good for their opinion.

At Sir Henry's request, Umbopa stood up. He was nearly six

feet tall and strongly built. Sir Henry walked up to him and looked into his proud, fine face.

'They make a good pair, don't they?' said Good.

'I like your looks, Mr Umbopa, and I will take you as my servant,' said Sir Henry in English.

Umbopa seemed to understand him, as he answered in Zulu, 'It is good.' And then he added, with a look at the white man's great height and strength, 'We are men, you and I.'

◆

I do not intend to describe our long journey up to Sitanda's Kraal, nearly a thousand miles from Durban. We started at the end of January and did not arrive until the second week of May. When we reached Inyati, a village in the Matabele country, we left the wagon and the cattle with our driver and leader. We left them because the bite of the tsetse fly is death to cattle and horses. Then, with Umbopa, Khiva, Ventvogel and six other men, we travelled the last 300 miles on foot.

One evening a number of deer ran past our camp and stopped in some trees about 300 feet away. Good went to look at them, followed by Khiva. We sat down and waited for them to return.

The sun was just going down, when suddenly we heard the scream of an elephant. The next moment we saw Good and Khiva running back to us. The huge elephant was coming after them. We picked up our guns but for a moment we could not shoot because they were in our way. Then a terrible thing happened. Good fell and went down on his face in front of the elephant.

We shouted and ran as fast as we could towards him. But Khiva had seen Good fall, and he stopped and turned. Then he threw his spear straight into the elephant's face.

With a scream of pain, the animal caught the poor Zulu and threw him to the earth. Then, placing his huge foot on his back, he pulled his body into two pieces. We fired our guns again and

Then he threw his spear straight into the elephant's face.

again, until the elephant fell down dead beside poor Khiva's body.

Good got up. For a long time he stood and looked at the man who had given his life for him. Umbopa also looked, then said, 'Ah well, he is dead, but he died like a man.'

We put the pieces of Khiva's body in a hole made by an animal, with a spear to protect him on his journey to a better world. The next day we continued marching, and at last we reached Sitanda's Kraal.

On the first evening, Good looked after the arrangements of our little camp, while Sir Henry and I walked to the top of a small hill and gazed across the desert. Far, far away I could see the faint blue form of the Suliman Mountains.

'There,' I said, 'there is the wall round Solomon's mines. God knows if we will ever climb it.'

'My brother may be there, and if he is, I'll reach him,' said Sir Henry.

'I hope so,' I answered, and I turned to go back to the camp. Then I saw that we were not alone. Behind us, also gazing at the mountains, stood Umbopa.

'Is that the land where you want to go?' he said, pointing towards the mountains with his spear.

'Yes, Umbopa,' answered Sir Henry.

'The desert is wide and there is no water in it. The mountains are high and covered with snow. And man cannot say what lies behind them. It is a long journey.'

'Yes,' answered Sir Henry, 'it is. But I am going to find my brother. And a man can make any journey on this earth if his heart wants it enough.'

'Great words, my father,' answered Umbopa. 'Perhaps I too will find a brother over the mountains.'

I looked at him. 'What do you mean? What do you know about those mountains?'

'A little. There is a strange land over there, a land of witches and beautiful things, a land of brave people and of trees, and streams, and snow mountains, and a great white road. I have heard of it.'

Chapter 4 Into the Desert

Next day we made our arrangements.

We took with us five rifles, three revolvers, five water-bottles, six pounds of sun-dried meat, our knives, some medicine, some matches and a few other things.

Three men from the village agreed to come with us for the first eighteen miles, carrying large pots of water. Then we could fill our water-bottles again after the first night's march.

We started in the cool of the evening. Our only guides were the mountains and old José da Silvestra's map. If we failed to find the 'pool of bad water' that his map showed in the middle of the desert, we would probably die of thirst.

We marched as silently as shadows through the night and in the heavy sand. It was very quiet and we felt alone.

At last daylight came and about an hour later we saw some rocks. The large shadow of one big piece of rock hung over the sand, and it allowed us to escape from the heat of the sun. We drank some water and ate a piece of dried meat. Then we lay down and were soon asleep.

It was three o'clock in the afternoon before we woke. The water-carriers were preparing to return home; they had seen enough of the desert already. So we drank, filled our water-bottles and then watched them leave. At half-past four we also started.

At sunset we stopped and waited for the moon. Then we marched through the night until the sun came up. We drank a little, and lay down on the sand to sleep. There was no escape from the heat of the sun. I do not know how we lived through the day. At three we began to move forward again.

At sunset we rested and got more sleep. When the moon came up, we marched again. We were suffering terribly from thirst. We did not have the strength to speak.

At two o'clock we stopped near a little hill and drank our last water. Then we lay down.

I heard Umbopa say to himself, 'If we cannot find water, we will all be dead before the moon appears tomorrow.'

After two hours, I woke up. The others were just beginning to wake.

'If we can believe Silvestra's map, there must be some water near here,' I said. No one seemed interested in this. It was clear that we could not be very sure of the map.

I saw Ventvogel walking about. Then he lifted his nose and seemed to smell the air.

'I smell water,' he said.

Just then, the sun came up. There, not more than fifty miles away, we saw Sheba's Breasts. The great Suliman Mountains stretched away for hundreds of miles on each side of them.

Sir Henry stroked his yellow beard thoughtfully. 'Perhaps there's water on the top of the hill,' he said.

'Rubbish,' said Good. 'When have you ever found water on the top of a hill?'

'Let's go and look,' I said.

We climbed up the sandy sides of the little hill – and there, in a deep hole, was water! It was black and did not look very clean, but it was water. We drank and drank, then we took off our clothes and sat down in it.

We stayed on the hill all day, waiting for the sun to go down. Then we drank again, filled our water-bottles, and started to walk.

◆

We stayed on the hill all day, waiting for the sun to go down.

Our water was finished again when we reached the foot of the mountain, but by good fortune we found some fruit. As we climbed, we suffered terribly during the nights from cold. We had little strength now, and no food.

On 23rd May, we climbed slowly up through the snow, lying down sometimes to rest. At sunset we were just below Sheba's left breast.

'We must be somewhere near the cave that the old gentleman wrote about,' said Good.

'Yes,' I said, 'if there is a cave. And if we do not find it before dark, we are dead men.'

We marched in silence. Then Umbopa stopped.

'Look!' he said. He pointed at a hole in the snow. 'It is the cave.'

We crept inside the cave, and sat close together. We could not sleep; the cold was too terrible.

At last the air began to grow grey with light. The sun looked in on our half-frozen bodies – and also on Ventvogel, who was sitting there dead among us.

Shocked, we stood up and moved away from his dead body. Then I heard a cry of fear from somebody, and turned my head. Sitting at the end of the cave, there was another body. The head rested on its chest, and the long arms hung down. I stared at it. It too was a dead man – and a white man. The body was completely frozen.

'José da Silvestra, of course,' said Good.

'Impossible!' I cried. 'He died 300 years ago.'

'Why not? He is frozen hard. Look, here is the piece of bone that he drew the map with.'

'Yes,' said Sir Henry, 'and here is the place where he took his blood to draw it with.' He pointed to a small cut on the left arm of the body.

We left those two, da Silvestra and poor Ventvogel, and crept out of the cave into the sunshine. How many hours would it be before we were like them?

Chapter 5 Solomon's Road

We walked to the edge of the mountain. The clouds had cleared a little. Below us, where the snow ended, we saw some green grass and a stream. A group of large deer stood by the stream. There was plenty of food if we could get it.

Sir Henry, Good and I aimed very carefully. 'Fire!' said Umbopa, in Zulu. As the smoke cleared away, we saw a great animal lying on its back.

But then we had a problem. There was no wood for a fire to cook the meat on. We looked at each other.

'We must eat it uncooked,' said Sir Henry. 'We are hungry, and there is no other way.'

So we ate, and our life and strength seemed to return. We began to look around. About 6,000 feet below us lay a great area of the most beautiful country I have ever seen. There was a thick forest, and a great silver river. To the left we could see hundreds of cattle on rich grassland. To the right were hills, with fields between them.

We sat and gazed in silence at this wonderful view. Then Sir Henry spoke. 'That must be Solomon's great road,' he said.

It was a fine road, cut out of the rock, at least fifty feet wide. We found a way down to it and began to march along it.

At midday we came to a wood and a small stream. We had a meal and rested. After some time I noticed that Good was not there, but then I saw him sitting by the bank of the stream. He had only his shirt on. He was brushing his clothes, shaking his head sadly at the state of them. He cleaned his shoes, and then began to brush his hair. Suddenly I saw a shining light pass by his head.

Good and I jumped up with a shout. A group of men had come from among the trees.

They were very tall. Some of them wore black feathers on their heads and had short coats of skins. A young man of about seventeen had thrown the spear. As I looked, an old man stepped forward, caught the young one's arm, and said something to him. Then they came towards us.

Sir Henry, Good and Umbopa picked up their rifles, but the men continued walking. Perhaps they did not know what rifles were.

'Put down your guns!' I shouted to the others.

Walking forward, I spoke to the old man. I did not know what language I should use.

'Greetings,' I said in Zulu. To my surprise, I was understood.

'Greetings,' answered the man, using a word that was not quite the same. We discovered later that these people spoke a very old form of Zulu. 'Where have you come from?' he continued. 'Why are three of your faces white, and the other face like ours?' He pointed to Umbopa. His face was very similar to the faces of the men in front of us.

'We are strangers, and come in peace,' I answered.

'You are lying,' he replied. 'No strangers can cross the mountains. But your lies are not important. No strangers can live in the land of the Kukuanas. It is the king's law. You must die, strangers.'

The hands of some of the men moved down to the great knives at their sides.

'Oh, Lord!' murmured Good. When he was anxious, he often put his hand to his false teeth, pulled down the top teeth and let them fly back into place. Fortunately, he did this now. The Kukuanas shouted in terror and ran back a little way.

'What is the matter?' I wondered.

'He moved his teeth,' whispered Sir Henry excitedly. 'Take them out, Good!'

Good obeyed, hiding the teeth in his hand.

The men came forward slowly – interested, but afraid.

'Why, strangers, does this fat man have clothes on his body but none on his legs?' asked the old man, pointing to Good. 'Why does he have one shining eye, and teeth that move?'

‘Open your mouth,’ I said to Good, and Good smiled. He showed a mouth that was as toothless as a new-born baby’s.

‘Where are his teeth?’ they shouted.

Good passed his hand across his mouth, then he opened his lips and there were his teeth again.

‘I see that you are not human,’ said the old man. ‘No man has a round shining eye, or teeth that move, and disappear, and grow again! Pardon us, my lords.’

‘We are men like you,’ I said, ‘but we come from another world. We come from the biggest star that shines at night.’

‘Oh! Oh!’ they cried.

‘We have come to stay with you for a time, and to help you. Now, what should we do to the man who threw a spear?’

‘Do not kill him, my lords,’ said the old man. ‘He is the king’s son.’

‘Perhaps,’ I said, ‘you do not think that we can kill him? You!’ I cried to Umbopa, ‘Give me the magic pipe that speaks.’ Umbopa smiled and handed me a rifle. ‘You see that deer,’ I said, pointing to an animal about 200 feet away. ‘Can a man kill it from here with a noise?’

‘It is not possible, my lord,’ answered the old man.

‘But I shall kill it,’ I said, quietly.

The old man smiled. ‘My lord cannot do that,’ he said.

I pointed the rifle at the deer. It was a small animal, and quite far away. I knew that I must not miss it. I took a deep breath and fired the gun. The deer jumped into the air and fell dead.

There was a cry of terror from the group of men.

‘If you want meat,’ I said, ‘fetch that deer.’

The old man made a sign. One of the men left, and returned with the deer. I had hit it in the right place, just behind the shoulder. They all looked at the hole in the poor animal’s body.

‘You see,’ I said, ‘I do not speak empty words.’

‘We are satisfied,’ said the old man. ‘All our witches cannot do a thing like that. Listen, Children of the Stars, Children of the Shining Eye and Disappearing Teeth, who kill from far away. I am Infadoos, son of Kafa, who was once king of the Kukuana people. This young man is Scragga, son of Twala, the great king, lord of the Kukuanas, keeper of the Great Road, terror of his enemies, leader of a hundred thousand soldiers, Twala the One-eyed, the Black, the Terrible.'

'Really?' I said. 'Lead us, then, to Twala.'

The old man bent his head and murmured the words, '*Koom, koom*,' which I afterwards discovered was their royal greeting. He then turned and spoke to his followers. They carried all our things – except the rifles, which they were afraid of.

Chapter 6 We Enter Kukuanaland

'Infadoos,' I said as we walked, 'who made this road?'

'It was made, my lord, many years ago. Nobody knows how or when – not even the wise woman, Gagool, who has lived for hundreds of years.'

'Has the king many soldiers?' I asked.

'When Twala calls all his soldiers, they cover the land.'

'Has there been a war recently?'

'There was a war years ago among ourselves. It is our custom that, when two sons are born at the same time, the weaker must die. The king, years ago, had two sons born together. Kafa was stronger. Everyone thought that Twala, the weaker son, was dead. Kafa became king. When he died, his oldest son, Imotu, was made king. But Gagool, the wise and terrible woman, had hidden Twala and now she brought him out. Twala killed Imotu, but Imotu's wife escaped with her baby, Ignosi. Nobody has seen her.'

'Then, if this child, Ignosi, is alive, he is the true king of the Kukuana people?' I said.

'Yes. The eldest son of the king is marked at birth by a great snake round his waist. We know him by that. If he is alive, he is king – but he must be dead.'

Umbopa was walking just behind me, listening with great interest.

A message had gone ahead of us. In the early afternoon we reached a village. As we came to it we saw large groups of soldiers marching out from its gates. They ran quickly up the hill towards us with shining spears and waving feathers, and made a line on each side of the road. Then, when we came closer, the royal greeting '*Koom*!' came from hundreds of throats.

These men were known as the Greys, from the colour of their shields. They were the finest soldiers of the Kukuana nation, and Infadoos was their leader.

As we passed, the Greys followed us. They marched with a regular step that shook the ground.

At sunset, from the top of some hills, we saw the city of Loo, capital of Kukuanaland. It was a very large place, five miles round. Near it was a hill with a strange shape, like a half-moon. A hundred miles beyond it stood three mountains. Their tops were sharp, unlike the round tops of Sheba's Breasts, and there was snow on them.

Infadoos saw us looking at these mountains and said, 'The road ends there. The mountains are full of caves. There the wise men of old time used to go. There our dead kings are now taken to the Place of Death.'

After an hour we reached the edge of the town and came to a great gate. Infadoos spoke, and we passed through into the main street. He led us past lines of huts to the gate of a group of huts. We were glad to eat and then sleep; we were very tired after our long journey.

◆

When we woke, the sun was high in the heavens. Infadoos told us that Twala the king was ready to see us.

We took a rifle and some presents for the king and walked a short distance to a very large square. It was filled by seven or eight thousand soldiers. The space in front of a large hut was empty, but facing it there were several seats. At a sign from Infadoos, we sat down.

At last the door of the hut opened and a huge man stepped out, followed by the boy, Scragga, and a kind of animal in a hairy coat. The king sat down and Scragga stood behind him. The animal crept into the shadow of the hut.

There was silence.

Then the king stood up. He had the most frightening face that we had ever seen. He had one angry black eye. The other eye had gone and there was only a hole in his face where it had been. It was a very cruel face, bad in every way. Around his head were a number of white feathers. His body was covered with shining armour. In his right hand was a large spear. On his forehead shone a huge diamond.

Still there was silence, but not for long. The king held up the great spear in his hand and eight thousand spears were lifted in answer. From eight thousand throats came the royal cry of '*Koom*'.

There was silence again, then it was broken. A soldier on our left dropped his shield.

Twala turned his cold eye in the direction of the noise.

'Come here, you,' he said, in a voice like thunder.

A young man stepped out and stood in front of him.

'Will you embarrass me in the eyes of these strangers from the stars? Speak!'

'It was an accident,' he murmured.

'Then you must pay for your accident. Scragga, kill this dog for me.'

Scragga stepped forward. He waved the spear once, twice,

On his forehead shone a huge diamond.

and then struck. The young soldier threw up his hands and dropped dead.

'It was a good stroke,' said the king. 'Take him away.'

Four men carried away the body of the murdered man.

Sir Henry was red with anger. 'Sit down!' I whispered.

Twala sat silently until the body had been carried away. Then he said, 'White people, where have you come from, and what do you want?'

'We come from the stars,' I answered. 'We have come to see this land.'

'Remember that the stars are far away and you are near. Why should we not kill you?'

I laughed – though not in my heart. 'Haven't they told you how I can kill from a distance?' I said.

'They have told me, but I do not believe them. Kill one of those men over there for me.'

'No,' I answered. 'We do not kill except to punish. But bring a cow in through the gates and I will strike it dead.'

'It will be done,' he said.

'Now, Sir Henry,' I said, 'you must shoot. We want to show that I am not the only one.' I gave him the rifle.

There was a pause. Then we saw a cow coming through the gate. It saw the great crowd of people and it stopped.

'Now!' I whispered.

There was a sharp sound, and the animal lay dead.

A whisper of surprise spread through the crowd.

Then I saw the animal-like figure creeping out from the shadow of the hut. When it reached the place where the king sat, I saw its face. It was the face of a very old woman, covered with deep yellow lines. This was Gagool, the witch, who was older than anybody's living memory.

She placed her hand on the shoulder of Twala the king and began to speak: 'Listen, King! Listen, soldiers! Listen, men and women! Listen. There is magic in me, and I tell you what will come.' Terror seemed to fill the hearts of all the people. 'Blood! Blood! Blood! Rivers of blood everywhere. I am old! I am old! Your fathers knew me, and their fathers' fathers. I have seen blood. Ha! ha! But I will see more before I die.

'What do you want, White Men of the Stars? Have you come for white stones? You will find them when the blood is dry. But will you then go away, or will you stay with me? Ha! ha! ha!

'And you with the dark proud face' – she pointed her finger at Umbopa – 'who are you? I think I know. I think I can smell the blood in your heart. Take off that cloth–'

She suddenly fell, fainting, to the ground.

The king stood up and waved his hand. The soldiers began to march away.

'White people,' the king said, 'perhaps I should kill you. Gagool has spoken strange words.'

I laughed. 'Be careful, King. We are not easy to kill.'

He put his hand to his forehead and thought.

'Go in peace,' he said at last. 'Tonight is a great dance. You must see it. Tomorrow I will decide.'

Chapter 7 The Witches

I asked Infadoos to enter our hut with us.

'Infadoos,' I said, 'it seems to us that Twala the king is a cruel man.'

'Yes, my lords. He does cruel things, and the land cries out. Tonight you will see. The witches will choose people and they will die. If the king wants to take a man's cattle or his wife, or if he fears a man, that man will die. Gagool or the other witches will find him. The land is tired of Twala and his bloody ways.'

'Then why, Infadoos, don't the people get rid of him?'

'If he were killed, Scragga would rule in his place. The heart of Scragga is blacker than the heart of Twala his father. When Imotu was killed, and then Ignosi his son died, all hope died with them.'

'No,' said Umbopa.

'What do you mean, boy?' asked Infadoos.

'Listen, Infadoos,' was the answer. 'Years ago the king, Imotu, was killed in this country, and his wife ran away with the boy Ignosi. The mother and the boy did not die. They crossed the mountains and were led by desert-men across the sands, until they came to water and trees again.'

'You are mad to talk like that,' said the old soldier.

'Do you think so? Look, I will show you, uncle.'

Then, with a single movement, Umbopa took off his cloth and stood in front of us.

'Look,' he said, and he pointed to the picture of a great snake marked in his skin around his waist.

Infadoos looked with open eyes, then fell on his knees.

'*Koom*! *Koom*!' he cried. 'It is my brother's son. It is the king.'

'Stand up, Infadoos. I am not yet king, but with your help, and with the help of my brave white friends, I shall be. But the old witch Gagool was right. There will be rivers of blood, and her blood must join it, if she has any. She killed my father with her words and pushed my mother away. Now, Infadoos, choose. Will you be my man?'

The old man got up and moved to Umbopa – or Ignosi. Then he took his hand.

'Ignosi, true king of the Kukuanas,' he said, 'I am your man until death. When you were a baby I played with you on my knees. Now my old arm will strike for you and we will free the land.'

'And you, white men, will you help me? What can I offer you? The white stones? If I win and can find them, you can have as many as you can carry away. Is that enough?'

I translated what he had said into English.

'Tell him,' Sir Henry said, 'that money is good, but a gentleman does not sell himself for money. But I have always liked Umbopa, and I do not like Twala, so I will help him.'

'Well,' said Good, 'I enjoy a good fight, so I am his man too.'

I repeated these answers in Zulu, and added, 'Umbopa, or Ignosi, I am a man of peace, and not very brave. But I support my friends and I will support you. I do need money, so I shall accept your offer of those diamonds. Now tell me – how do you intend to become king?'

'I do not know,' replied Ignosi. 'Infadoos, have you a plan?'

'Tonight,' answered Infadoos, 'the witches will work and there will be anger in the hearts of many people against King Twala. When the dance ends, I will speak to some of the great chiefs. I will bring them here and show them that you are the real king. I think that by tomorrow you will have 20,000 spears at your command.'

At that moment our talk was interrupted by the king's messengers. Three men entered the hut. Each man carried a shining shirt of chain armour and a fine battle-axe, gifts from the king.

That night, when the full moon shone, Infadoos arrived in armour with a guard of twenty men. He asked us to put on the shirts of chain armour under our other clothes. We took our revolvers to the dance.

The great square was filled with about 20,000 men. Not a sound came from them.

'They are very silent,' said Good.

'What does he say?' asked Infadoos. I told him. 'Men are silent in the shadow of Death,' he answered quietly.

'Tell me,' I asked Infadoos, 'are we in danger?'

'I do not know, my lords. I hope not. But you must not seem afraid. If you live through the night, you may live. The soldiers are murmuring against the king.'

A small group came from the direction of the royal hut.

'It is the king, and Scragga his son, and Gagool, and the men who kill.' Infadoos pointed to ten huge men carrying spears.

'Look around, white lords,' said Twala, and he moved his one cruel eye along the soldiers. 'There are men there who have bad things in their hearts and fear the judgement.'

'Begin! Begin!' cried Gagool, in her thin voice.

Strange and terrible figures ran towards us. They were old women. Their white hair flew out behind them as they ran. Their faces were painted with lines of white and yellow, and each woman held a bent stick in her hand. They stopped in front of Gagool and cried, 'Old Mother, we are here.'

'Then go! The killers' spears are sharp. Go!'

Gagool's terrible pupils ran in every direction. We could not watch them all, so we fixed our eyes on the witch who was nearest to us. When she came near the soldiers, she began to dance wildly, turning round and round, and crying, 'I can smell him, the bad one.'

She danced more and more quickly until suddenly she stopped, like a hunting dog that smells something. Then with an angry cry she touched a tall soldier with her stick. The two men next to him held the unhappy man, and moved with him towards the king. Two of the killers stepped forward to meet him.

'Kill,' said the king.

'Kill,' cried Gagool.

Almost before the words were spoken, the terrible thing was done.

Another poor fellow was brought out almost immediately after this, and so the game of death continued. Once we stood up and tried to stop it, but Twala refused to listen.

At last the witches seemed to become tired of their bloody work, but they had not finished. To our surprise, Gagool stood up and moved forward. This horrible yellow-headed old woman slowly grew stronger until at last she danced almost as quickly as her terrible pupils. Suddenly she ran at a tall man and touched him. As she did this, we heard a shout from the men that he commanded. We learnt later that he was a rich and powerful man, a cousin of the king.

Then Gagool came nearer and nearer to us.

'Who will it be?' murmured Sir Henry.

Then she rushed to Umbopa and touched him on the shoulder. 'Kill him!' she cried. 'He is a bad man. Kill him, the stranger, before there are rivers of blood.'

I stood up. 'This man,' I shouted, 'is a servant of the king's guests. Whoever harms him harms us. We are your guests, and I demand protection for him.'

'He must die,' was the angry answer.

'He will not die,' I replied. 'Whoever tries to touch him will die.'

'Take him!' Twala shouted to the killers who stood around. They were red with the blood of the dead.

'Stand back!' I shouted. 'Stand back if you want to see tomorrow's light. If you touch him, your king will die.' I pointed my revolver at Twala. Sir Henry and Good also pulled out their revolvers. Sir Henry pointed his at the leading killer and Good aimed carefully at Gagool.

Twala stepped back.

'Well,' I said, 'what do you think, Twala?'

He spoke. 'You have said that he is my guest. For that reason, and not from fear of you, I will not kill him.'

'I am glad,' I answered quietly. 'We are tired of death and want to sleep. Has the dance ended?'

'It has ended,' said Twala in an angry voice.

He lifted his spear. The soldiers began to march away through the gateway in perfect silence.

Chapter 8 We Give a Sign

It was almost morning when Infadoos came to us, followed by six fine-looking chiefs.

'My lords and Ignosi, true king of the Kukuanas, I have brought these men with me. They are great men and each has command of 3,000 soldiers. Now let them also see the mark of the great snake and hear your story. Then they will say if they will join you against Twala the king.'

Ignosi took off the cloth and showed the mark. Each chief came near and examined it by the low light of the lamp. Then Ignosi put on his cloth again, and repeated his story.

Infadoos said, 'Will you help this man to be king, as his father was? The land is crying out against Twala and the people's blood is pouring like rain.'

The oldest of the six men, who was short with white hair, stepped forward and answered, 'Your words are true, Infadoos. The land is crying out. My own brother died tonight. But how do we know that this is the real king? There will be rivers of blood before this ends, because many people will fight for Twala. If this man really is the king, he must give us a sign that everyone can see.'

'You have seen the sign of the snake,' I answered.

'That is not enough. Perhaps the snake was put there after his birth. We will do nothing without a sign.'

The other chiefs agreed. I turned to Sir Henry and Good and explained the situation.

'I think I know what to do,' Good said. 'Ask them to give us a moment to think.'

I did, and the chiefs left the room. Good went to the little box where he kept his medicines. He took out a diary. 'Now,' he said, 'isn't tomorrow the fourth of June?'

We had counted the days carefully, and it was.

'Good – "4th June, total eclipse of the moon, can be seen in Tenerife, *Africa* . . ." There is a sign for you. Tell them that you will make the moon dark tomorrow night.'

'And if the diary is wrong?' Sir Henry said to Good, who was writing some numbers on another page.

'Eclipses are usually on time,' answered Good. 'I do not know our exact position, but it will begin at about ten o'clock tomorrow night and end at half-past twelve. For an hour and a half it will be totally dark.'

'Well,' said Sir Henry, 'I cannot think of a better idea.'

I could not either, so I asked Umbopa to bring the chiefs back.

'Great men of the Kukuanas, listen.' I said. 'We do not enjoy showing our power, but this is important and we are angry with the king. Tell me – can any man stop the moon and make the land dark?'

The chiefs laughed at this, and the oldest one said, 'No man can do that.'

'Tomorrow night, two hours before midnight, we will make the moon disappear for an hour and a half. Darkness will cover the earth. If we do this, will you believe that Ignosi is the real king of the Kukuanas?'

'Yes,' the old chief said, and the others agreed. 'If you do this, we will be satisfied.'

Then Infadoos spoke. 'Two miles from Loo,' he said to us, 'there is a hill shaped like a half-moon. If you really can make the moon dark, I will lead you out of Loo to that place. There you will be safe. And from there we can make war on Twala the king.'

'Good,' I said. 'Now, let us sleep and make our magic.'

'I hope that this eclipse happens,' Sir Henry said, after they had gone.

'If it does not happen,' I answered, 'it will be the last moon that we will ever see.'

◆

The next evening we put on the chain armour from the king and went to the great square in front of the king's hut with our rifles. The square looked very different from the evening before. Kukuana girls were wearing flowers in their hair. Each girl carried a large leaf in one hand and a tall white flower in the other. In the centre of the open space Twala the king sat, with old Gagool at his feet. The boy Scragga and twelve guards were also there.

Twala greeted us and seemed happy, although he looked hard at Umbopa. Then, 'The dance will begin,' he said, and the girls moved forward. They danced and sang, waving the leaves and flowers. At last they stopped, and an attractive young woman stepped forward and danced alone. When she became tired, another woman took her place, and then another and another.

The king held up his hand. 'Which of these girls do you think is the most attractive?' he asked us.

'The first,' I said, without thinking.

'Then my mind is the same as your mind and my eyes are like your eyes. She is the prettiest, and that is a bad thing for her because she must die!'

'*Yes, must die!*' said Gagool.

'But why?' I said. 'She has danced well.'

Twala laughed as he answered. 'It is our custom, and she belongs to those stone figures.' He pointed towards the three mountains. 'If I do not kill the girl, bad luck will come to my people.'

Then, turning to the guards, he said, 'Bring her here.'

The girl cried out and tried to run away. But two men caught her and brought her to the king.

'What is your name, girl?' said Gagool. 'Will you not answer? Must the king's son do his work now?'

Scragga stepped forward and lifted his great spear. At the same time I saw Good's hand creep to his revolver.

'Mother,' the girl answered, and her voice was shaking, 'my

name is Foulata. Why must I die? I have done no wrong.'

Good made an angry noise and moved towards the girl, and she threw her arms around him.

'Father from the stars,' she said, 'protect me!'

'Yes, yes, of course,' Good said.

Twala made a sign to his son, who moved forward.

'What are you waiting for?' Sir Henry whispered to me.

'I am waiting for something to happen,' I said. 'I have been watching the moon for half an hour and it looks completely normal.'

'Well, you must take a chance now, or the girl will be killed,' he said.

I stepped between the girl and Scragga's spear. 'King,' I said, 'we will not allow this.'

Twala stood up angrily. There was a murmur from the chiefs.

'*Will not allow this*?' he said. 'Are you mad? How can you stop it? Scragga, kill her. Guards! Take these men.'

As the guard moved towards us, Sir Henry, Good and Umbopa lifted their rifles.

'Stop!' I said. 'Stop! We will *not* allow this. And to show my power, I will make the moon dark.'

The men stopped, and we all looked up. I was happy to see that we had made no mistake. There was a small shadow on the edge of the moon, and the light was already less bright. I lifted my hand towards the sky and began to repeat a poem. Sir Henry remembered some Shakespeare, and Good said all the bad words that he had ever heard at sea.

Slowly, a shadow crept over the moon, and a great cry of fear came from all the people.

'Look, King,' I cried. 'Look, Gagool! Look, chiefs and men and women. Do the white men from the stars keep their promise?'

'It will pass,' Gagool said. 'I have seen this thing before. No man can stop the moon. Just wait and it will pass.'

But nobody listened to her. The shadow moved across the moon, which turned blood-red. The people stood still, staring at the sky.

'The moon is dying – they have killed the moon,' the boy Scragga shouted out at last. 'We will all die in the dark.'

He lifted his spear and struck hard at Sir Henry's chest. But the spear hit Sir Henry's armour and did not hurt him. Before he could try again, Sir Henry took his spear and pushed it through him. Scragga fell down dead.

Then the girls ran screaming towards the gates. They were followed by the king, his guards, some chiefs and Gagool. We were left alone with Foulata and the chiefs who had spoken to us the night before.

'Now,' I said, 'we have given you a sign. If you believe us, let us run quickly to the place that you spoke about.'

'Come,' said Infadoos, turning to go.

We followed, and I saw that Good had taken Foulata's hand. It was now totally dark.

Chapter 9 The Battle

When the sun came up, we prepared for battle. We found Infadoos with his own men, the Greys. Ignosi joined us. The men were watching Twala's army marching out of Loo in a long line.

Infadoos and Ignosi spoke to the soldiers. They gave the royal greeting of '*Koom*', accepting Ignosi as their king.

'Infadoos, my uncle,' said Ignosi, 'you see how the hill bends round like a half-moon. The flat land runs like a green tongue towards us inside it. Your soldiers must go with another chief's men down to the green tongue. When Twala sees you, he will order his whole army to fight against you. But the place is narrow, and only one group of soldiers can attack. While the eyes of Twala's army are on the fight on the narrow tongue, the rest of our army will creep along the two sides of the half-moon. We will then attack Twala's army from both sides.'

The arrangements for the battle were made very quickly. The men ate a small meal and then marched to their places.

Then Good came to Sir Henry and myself. 'Goodbye,' he said. 'I am going to be with the people on the right, and we may not meet again.' We shook hands in silence.

'I shall be with the Greys,' said Sir Henry, 'and I do not expect to see tomorrow's sun. The Greys will have to fight until they are all dead, while the rest of the army gets round the sides. Well, it will be a man's death. Goodbye, old fellow.'

In another moment, Good had gone. Infadoos led Sir Henry to his place in the front line of the Greys. I went with Ignosi to my place with a second group, who were behind them.

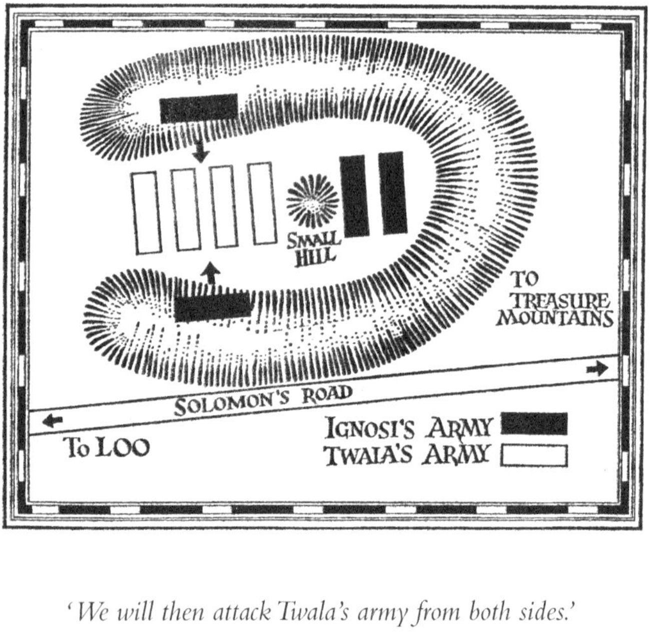

'We will then attack Twala's army from both sides.'

When we reached the edge of the hill, the Greys were already half-way down. Twala's army was now near. They had seen the movement of the Greys, and they were hurrying to reach the open end of the tongue before the Greys could come out on to the huge flat land. The Greys reached the centre of the tongue, where it became wider. There they stopped.

We moved down to a place about 300 feet behind them, on slightly higher ground.

Twala's army began to enter the valley. They discovered that the space was very narrow, and in front of them they saw the famous Greys, the best of the Kukuana army. Then Twala gave an order, and the first men ran towards the Greys.

The Greys did not move until the attackers were 130 feet away. Then suddenly, with a shout, they ran forward and the two lines met. The sound of the meeting shields came to our ears like thunder. The great group of battling men moved this way and that, but not for long. Suddenly the attacking lines began to grow thinner. Then, like a great wave over a rock, the Greys passed over them. But the Greys had only two lines left now. One third of them were dead.

They stood shoulder to shoulder, and waited for the second attack. I was glad to see Sir Henry's yellow beard as he moved among the men. So he was still alive!

The terrible thunder of shields came again. This time the fight was longer. We thought that the Greys were finished, and we were preparing to take their place. But then I heard the sound of Sir Henry's deep voice, and saw his battle-axe circling high above his head. The Greys stopped moving back. They stood like rock, as the waves of spearmen hit their shields again and again. Then they began to move forward, and suddenly the attackers were running away.

Less than a quarter of the Greys were still standing, but they shouted and waved their spears. Then they ran to a little piece of higher ground and formed three rings around it. There I saw Sir

. . . then I heard the sound of Sir Henry's deep voice, and saw his battle-axe circling high above his head.

Henry, unhurt, with our old friend Infadoos. Twala's soldiers moved towards them, and the battle began again.

'Are we going to stand here until we grow old, Ignosi, while Twala eats our brothers there?' I asked.

As I spoke, enemy soldiers rushed past the ring on the small hill and attacked it from the nearer side.

'Now is the moment,' cried Ignosi, and he lifted his battle-axe as the sign to attack.

I cannot describe what followed. I heard the sound of shouting voices, and saw shining spears through a red curtain of blood. When my mind cleared, I found myself inside the ring of the Greys, just behind Sir Henry.

Again and again they attacked us, and again and again we beat them back. But all the time our circle grew smaller. That old soldier, Infadoos, gave calm orders and stepped forward every time to the worst fighting. It was a fine sight.

Even finer was the sight of Sir Henry. Nobody lived where he struck.

An anxious cry came from the soldiers who were attacking us. Our men had moved round the sides and were attacking the enemy from all directions. As Ignosi had expected, all Twala's army had fixed their eyes on the bloody fight against the Greys. Then suddenly they realized, too late, what was happening.

In five minutes the result of the battle was decided. Twala's soldiers ran away. Soon the whole land between us and Loo was covered with groups of men, running from the battle-ground. The men around our circle disappeared, and we were left there with the dead and dying all around us. Only ninety-five of the brave Greys were still on their feet. More than 3,400 had fallen, most of them for the last time.

Chapter 10 Good Is Sick

We marched to Loo. When we arrived at the nearest gate, we found a group of our soldiers watching it. The officer in command of these men greeted Ignosi as king. Twala's army was, he said, inside the town, and Twala was there too. He said that they would probably not try to stop us. Ignosi sent a man forward to the gate, ordering the defenders to open it. He gave a royal promise of life and forgiveness to every man who put down his spear. Soon after this the gate was opened and we marched into the town.

Soldiers stood along the road. Their heads were bent, and their shields and spears lay at their feet. As Ignosi passed, they greeted him. We marched straight into the square and there, in front of his hut, sat Twala. Only one person was with him – Gagool. It was a sad sight.

As we moved towards him, Gagool shouted at us. Twala lifted his head and gazed at Ignosi. His one eye seemed to shine almost as brightly as the great diamond on his forehead.

'Greetings, King,' he said angrily. 'What have you decided to do with me?'

'The same as you did to my father,' was the answer.

'Good. But I will die fighting.'

Infadoos had told us that by Kukuana law a man of royal blood cannot be killed. He must choose one man after another man to fight him until one of them kills him.

'You have the right,' said Ignosi. 'Choose. Who will you fight? I cannot fight you, because a king only fights in war.'

Twala's eye looked up and down our line. I felt for a moment that it rested on me. What chance would I have against that huge man, nearly six feet tall?

Then Twala said, turning to Sir Henry, 'What do you say? Or are you afraid?'

'No,' said Ignosi quickly. 'You will not fight him.'

'Not if he is afraid,' said Twala.

Unfortunately Sir Henry understood these words, and the blood rushed into his face.

'I will fight him,' he said. 'No man will say that I am afraid. I am ready now.' He stepped forward and lifted his axe.

Twala laughed and stepped forward too. Then they began to circle round each other, holding their battle-axes up.

Suddenly Sir Henry jumped forward, but Twala stepped to one side. The stroke was a strong one, and the striker nearly fell forward after it. Twala quickly lifted his great battle-axe above his head and brought it down with terrible force. But with a quick movement of his left arm, Sir Henry brought his shield between himself and the axe. The axe cut the edge of the shield, and the axe fell on his left shoulder, but it did not do any serious damage. Sir Henry aimed a second stroke, which also hit Twala's shield. Then more attacks followed. The excited crowd shouted at every stroke.

Sir Henry caught a new stroke on his shield and then hit back with all his force. The stroke cut through Twala's shield and through the chain armour behind it, reaching his shoulder. With a cry of pain Twala returned the stroke, cutting through the handle of Sir Henry's battle-axe and then into his face.

A worried cry came from the crowd as the head of Sir Henry's axe fell to the ground. Twala lifted his axe again and rushed at him with a shout.

The next moment I saw Sir Henry's shield lying on the ground. Sir Henry had his great arms round Twala's waist. They moved this way and that way, using all their strength. Twala pushed Sir Henry off his feet and they fell together, turning over and over on the ground. Twala struck at Sir Henry's head with his battle-axe, and Sir Henry tried to push his knife through Twala's armour.

'Get his axe,' shouted Good, and perhaps Sir Henry heard

him. He dropped the knife and reached for the axe, which was tied to Twala's arm by a piece of leather. Still turning over and over, they fought for it like wild cats. Suddenly the leather string broke. Sir Henry got free, with the axe in his hand.

He jumped to his feet, the red blood pouring from the deep cut in his face. Twala was on his feet too. He pulled out a heavy knife and rushed straight at Sir Henry. He struck him on the breast, but the chain armour stopped the knife. He struck again, and again the knife was stopped. Then, lifting the big axe over his head, Sir Henry hit his enemy with all his force. There was a shout of excitement from a thousand throats. Twala's head fell from his shoulders, and Sir Henry fell heavily across the body of the dead king.

Sir Henry was carried into Twala's hut. He woke up soon, but we were all very tired and our bodies hurt from the fighting. With Foulata's help, we took off the chain armour and lay down. Sir Henry and Good both had many cuts, and Good had lost a lot of blood from a deep cut in his leg. Foulata brought some leaves, which reduced the pain, and Good used some medicine from his own box. We ate soup and lay down to sleep.

When we woke up in the morning, after a difficult night, Good had a high fever and blood was coming from his mouth. Foulata tried to help him.

Later in the day, Ignosi held a great meeting. He was recognized as king by all the chiefs. In front of the whole army, he thanked the few men of the Greys who were still alive. He gave each man a present of cattle, and he made them officers.

Afterwards we had a short visit from Ignosi, who now wore the royal diamond on his forehead.

'Greetings, King,' I said, standing up.

'Yes, king at last, with the help of you three great men,' he answered.

I asked him what he had decided to do with Gagool.

'I shall kill her,' he answered, 'and all the other witches with her. She has always taught the witches and brought problems to the land.'

'But she knows a lot,' I said. 'It is easier to destroy knowledge than to find it.'

'That is true,' he said. 'She knows the secret of the Silent Ones over there where the great road leads, and where the dead kings are taken.'

'Yes, and that is where the diamonds are. Do not forget your promise. You must lead us to the mines, even if Gagool has to stay alive to show the way.'

'I will not forget,' he said, 'and I will think about your words.'

After Ignosi left, I went to see Good. He was very ill. The fever was much worse, and it continued for four or five days. All this time Foulata stayed with him. At first I tried to help, and Sir Henry too, when he felt better. But Foulata told us to leave him with her. For two days I thought that he would die. Only Foulata did not believe it.

'He will live,' she said.

One night, the fifth night of his illness, I went to see him before I went to sleep. I entered the hut quietly. The lamp on the floor showed that Good was not moving. So it had happened at last! I made a noise like a soft cry.

'Sshhh,' came from a dark shadow behind Good's head.

Then, creeping closer, I saw that he was not dead. He was sleeping deeply, with Foulata's fingers in his hand. He slept like that for eighteen hours and all the time Foulata stayed with him.

When Good was nearly well again, Sir Henry told him how Foulata had saved his life. Good took me to the hut where she was preparing a meal. He asked me to translate his words into her language.

'Tell her,' he said, 'that I will never forget what she has done.'

After I repeated this in Zulu, she said to him, 'Have you

forgotten that you also saved my life?'

She had forgotten that Sir Henry and I also helped a little! I left them together. I knew that if their relationship continued, Good would have to stay there. A marriage between them was not possible outside Kukuanaland.

Chapter 11 The Place of Death

A few days later Ignosi called all the people together and they publicly recognized him as king. After this we spoke to him, and said that we now wanted to go to the mines.

'My friends,' he answered, 'I have discovered this. There is a great cave deep in the mountain where the dead kings of the land are put. There you will find Twala's body, with the kings who went before him. There, too, is a deep hole. That is where men found the valuable stones long ago. And there, in the Place of Death, is a secret room which is known only to Gagool.

'But there is a story in the land that many, many years ago a white man crossed the mountains. He was led by a woman to the secret room and he was shown the diamonds that are hidden in it. But the woman told the king about him, and he was chased back to the mountains.'

'The story is true, Ignosi. We found the white man,' I said.

'Yes, we found him,' answered Ignosi. 'And now, if you can reach that secret room, and the stones are there, you can take them, my brothers.'

'First we must find the secret room,' I said.

'There is only one person who can show it to you – Gagool,' he replied.

'And if she will not?'

'Then she must die,' answered Ignosi. 'I have saved her life for this.' He ordered two men to bring Gagool to him.

In a few minutes she came, shouting at her guards.

'Leave her,' said the king.

'What do you want, Ignosi?' she said. 'If you touch me, I will kill you with my magic.'

'Your magic could not save Twala, and it cannot hurt me,' was the answer. 'You must tell me the way to the secret room where the shining stones are hidden.'

'Ha! ha!' she cried. 'Nobody else knows its secret, and I will never tell you.'

Slowly Ignosi cut her with his spear.

'I will show it,' cried Gagool. 'Let me live and I will show you.'

'Tomorrow you will go with Infadoos and my white brothers. If you fail, you will die – slowly.'

'I will not fail, Ignosi. I always keep my promise. Once before, a woman showed the secret room to a white man, and bad things happened to him.' Her eyes shone. 'Her name was Gagool too. Perhaps I was that woman.'

'That was hundreds of years ago,' I said.

'Perhaps. Perhaps it was my mother's mother who told me. Her name was Gagool. You will find a bag full of stones in the place. The man filled the bag, but he never took it away. Bad luck came to him.'

◆

Our group contained the three of us, Foulata, Infadoos and Gagool. We marched along Solomon's great road to the foot of the middle hill, and stopped. Then, for an hour and a half, we climbed up a path. At last we saw in front of us a huge hole in the ground, about 300 feet deep.

'What is this?' Sir Henry wanted to know.

'This must be Solomon's diamond mine,' I said.

We moved closer to the three huge figures that we had seen on the other side of the mine. They were human shapes, cut out of the rock. These were the Silent Ones.

In front of us was a wall of rock about eighty feet high. Gagool carried a lamp in her hand. She gave us one bad look, then moved towards this wall. We followed her until we came to a narrow door.

'Now, white men from the stars,' she said, 'are you ready? I will obey the orders of my lord the king, and show you the place where the bright stones are kept.'

'We are ready,' I said.

'Good! Good! Your hearts must be strong. Are you coming too, Infadoos?'

'No,' replied Infadoos, 'it is not right for me to enter there. But be careful with my lords. If a hair of them is hurt, Gagool, you die. Do you hear?'

'I hear. I will obey the orders of the king. I have obeyed the orders of many kings, and in the end they obeyed mine. Ha! ha! I am going to look at their faces again now!'

Gagool went through the door. The three of us followed, and Foulata came too. The path was narrow, just wide enough for two people. When we had gone about 150 feet, we saw that the way was growing faintly light. A minute later we were in the most wonderful place that anyone has ever seen.

It was a huge cave. There were no windows, but a little light came in from above. Great columns stood at the sides, formed by water falling from the roof. The water carried salts, which in time became as hard as ice. High above us, hanging from the roof, we could see the points of huge icy needles.

Gagool led us straight to the end of the great silent cave, where we found another doorway.

'Are you ready to enter the Place of Death, white men?' asked Gagool.

'We are,' said Good, trying not to look afraid.

After about twenty steps we found ourselves in a room about

Great columns stood at the sides, formed by water falling from the roof.

forty feet long and thirty feet wide. It had been cut out of the mountain by the work of many hands. It was darker than the great cave, and at first I could only see a large stone table along the whole length of it. A huge white figure sat at one end of the table, and other figures sat around it.

My eyes began to see more clearly in the dark, and I saw a terrible sight. Death himself sat at the end of the table, holding a great white spear in his bony fingers. The figure was formed from human bones, and was about sixteen feet high. This must be the White Death in José da Silvestra's letter.

'What are those?' asked Good, pointing to the other figures round the table.

'Hee! hee! hee!' laughed Gagool. 'Bad luck comes to men who enter the Hall of the Dead. Hee! hee! Come and see the man you killed.'

The old woman caught Sir Henry's coat in her thin fingers and led him towards the table. We followed.

Then she stopped and pointed at the centre of the table. Sitting there, without clothes, was the body of Twala, the last king of the Kukuanas. Its head was on its knees. Over the body was a thin glassy covering which made it appear even more terrible. At first we could not understand this. Then we saw that the water fell slowly from the roof on to the neck and over the dead body. Like those wonderful columns and needles in the great cave, Twala's body was changing into stone!

I looked at the white forms round the stone table. They were human bodies once, now stone. There they sat for centuries, and for centuries they stayed the same.

Chapter 12 Solomon's Treasure House

'Now, Gagool,' I said in a low voice, 'lead us to the treasure room.'

'My lords are not afraid?' she said, looking up into my face.

'We are not.'

'Very good, my lords.' She went round to the back of great Death. 'Here is the room.'

She put her lamp on the floor and placed her hands against the side of the cave. I took a match and lit the lamp and then looked for the doorway. There was nothing in front of us except the wall of rock.

Gagool laughed. 'Look!' she said, and she pointed at the rock.

A large piece of stone was moving slowly up from the floor and disappearing into the rock above. Very slowly and gently the great stone lifted itself, until at last there was a dark hole in the place where it had been.

Our excitement was great. Was old da Silvestra right? Were there diamonds in that dark place, diamonds which would make us the richest men in the whole world?

'Enter, white men from the stars,' said Gagool, 'but first listen. The bright stones were taken from the hole where the Silent Ones sit. They were put here by someone – I do not know who. Only one person has entered this place since that time. Long ago a white man reached this country from over the mountains and was welcomed by that king.' She pointed to the fifth king at the Table of the Dead. 'A woman of this country had, by chance, learnt the secret of the door. The white man entered with this woman. He found the stones, and filled a bag with them. Then he took one more stone, a large one, and held it in his hand.' She paused.

'Well?' I asked. 'What happened to da Silvestra?'

The old woman seemed surprised. 'How do you know the dead man's name?' she asked quickly. Then without waiting for an answer, she continued: 'For some reason the white man became frightened. He threw down the bag, and ran out with that stone in his hand. And the king took the stone, the stone which Ignosi now wears.'

'Has nobody entered here since?' I asked.

'Nobody, my lords. Every king has opened it, but he has not entered. Death will come in one month to anyone who enters. Ha! Ha! Enter, my lords. If my words are true, the bag with the stones will lie on the floor. You will soon learn if it is true that death always follows. Ha! ha! ha!'

She went through the doorway, taking the lamp with her. We followed.

Just inside the door, Foulata said that she could not continue. She waited there. The rest of us followed Gagool. About fifty feet beyond the entrance we came to a painted wooden door. It was standing open. The last person there had not found the time, or had forgotten, to shut it.

In this doorway lay a bag that appeared to be full of stones.

'Hee! hee!' laughed Gagool, as the light from her lamp fell on it. 'I told you that the white man left quickly and dropped the bag. That is it!'

Good bent down and lifted it. 'I believe it *is* full of diamonds,' he whispered.

'Let's go in,' said Sir Henry. 'Here, give me the lamp.' He took it from Gagool's hand and stepped through the doorway.

We followed, and found ourselves in Solomon's treasure room. It was a room cut out of the rock, not more than ten feet square.

'My lords, look over there where it is darkest,' said Gagool. 'There are three stone boxes. Two are shut and one is open.'

We hurried across the room. There were three stone boxes against the wall. Sir Henry held the lamp over the open box. It was almost full of uncut diamonds. We stood and gazed at them.

'Hee! hee! hee!' laughed old Gagool behind us. 'There are

It was almost full of uncut diamonds.

the bright stones that you love. Take them in your fingers. Eat them, hee! hee! Drink them, ha! ha!'

We opened the other two boxes. The first of them was full to the top. The other was only about a quarter full, but these were the best stones. Some were as large as eggs.

We did not see the terrible look of hate on old Gagool's face as she crept out of the treasure-room towards the great door of rock.

Suddenly Foulata shouted. 'Oh, come quickly! Help! Help! The rock is falling.'

We started running. The light from the lamp showed us that the door of rock was closing slowly. It was less than a few feet from the floor. Near it, Gagool and Foulata were fighting. Foulata's blood was on the floor, but still she held the old witch. Then Gagool got free and threw herself on the ground to get under the closing stone. But the door caught her and she shouted in terrible pain. Down, down it came, the whole weight of it. We had never heard such horrible screams, and then the door was shut.

We turned to Foulata. She was badly hurt and I saw that she could not live for long. She looked up at Good, who was holding her in his arms. I heard her say that she loved him. Then she was silent.

'She is dead – she is dead!' said Good, and tears ran down his face.

'Well, we will soon join her, old fellow,' said Sir Henry. 'The door is shut, and this is where we will all die.'

◆

For a few minutes we stood there. All our strength had gone. This idea of our slow and terrible end silenced us. We understood now that the witch Gagool had planned this for us. Now I understood the meaning of her words about eating and drinking the diamonds. Perhaps someone had tried to do the same thing to poor old da Silvestra. That was why he had left in such a hurry, without his bag of jewels.

'We must do something,' said Sir Henry. 'The lamp will soon go out. Where is the handle that moves the rock?'

We began to feel up and down the door and the rock at the sides. But we could discover nothing.

'I am sure,' I said, 'that it cannot be opened from the inside. Gagool rushed to get underneath the stone.'

'We can do nothing with the door,' said Sir Henry. 'Let's go back to the treasure room.'

We sat down with our backs against the three stone boxes of diamonds. We had brought a basket of food and some water with us. There was enough food and water for about two days.

We ate and drank and felt a little better. Then we got up and began to examine the walls and floor of our prison. There was no way out. It was unlikely that there would be a second entrance to a treasure room.

'Quatermain,' said Sir Henry, 'what is the time?'

I looked to see. It was six o'clock. We had entered the cave at eleven.

'Infadoos will miss us,' I said. 'If we do not return tonight, he will search for us in the morning.'

'He does not know the secret of the door,' replied Sir Henry. 'He does not even know where it is. And if he found the door, he could not break it down. There are several feet of rock.'

The flame of the lamp became smaller. Then it burned bright for a moment and showed the whole scene: the soft shine of the diamonds, and the white faces of the three men who were waiting for death.

Suddenly, the flame went out.

Chapter 13 We Lose Hope

I cannot give a real description of the night that followed. We were prisoners in the centre of a great snow-topped mountain. Thousands of feet above us the fresh air rushed over the white snow, but no sound reached us. More than three feet of rock separated us from the awful Hall of the Dead, and the dead make no noise. The silence was total.

Enough treasures lay around us for a whole nation, but we could not buy the smallest chance of escape. We could not change them for a little food or a cup of water, or for a quick end to our suffering.

'Good,' said Sir Henry's voice at last, and it sounded terrible in that great silence, 'how many matches have you got in the box?'

'Eight.'

'Strike one and let's see the time.'

After that black darkness, the flame nearly blinded us. It was five o'clock. The early morning sun was now shining on the snow far above our heads.

'Let's eat,' said Sir Henry. 'While there is life there is hope.'

So we ate and then drank a little water.

After some time we went to the door and shouted. Good, from long practice at sea, made a terrible noise. I had never heard such shouts, but there was nobody there.

So we sat down against the boxes of useless diamonds. There was nothing that we could do.

Brave Sir Henry Curtis tried to help. He told stories of men who had made wonderful escapes. And when these failed to make us happier, he reminded us that death must come to us all. It would be quick and easy, he said (which was not true).

And so the day continued – if 'day' is the right word for the blackest night. When we lit a match to see the time, it was seven o'clock.

We ate and drank again, and then an idea came to me.

'How,' I said, 'does the air in this place stay fresh?'

'You are right!' said Good. 'I never thought of that! It cannot come through the stone door. It must come from somewhere. If no air was coming in, we would not be able to breathe now. Let's have a look.'

In a moment we were all creeping about on our hands and knees, feeling for the slightest sign of air. After an hour or two Sir Henry and I gave up, but Good still continued. It was better, he said, than doing nothing.

'Here, you fellows!' he said, after some time, in an excited voice. 'Quatermain, put your hand where mine is. Now can you feel anything?'

'I think I feel air coming up.'

'Now listen.' He jumped on the place and hope grew in our hearts because the sound was hollow.

With shaking hands I lit a match. As it burned, we examined the spot. There was a narrow space in the rock floor, and – a stone ring.

We were too excited to speak. Good had a knife. He opened it and moved it round the ring. Finally he got the knife under it and pressed gently up. Soon he could put his hands into it. He pulled and pulled, but nothing moved.

'Let me try,' I said. I held it and pulled, but with no result.

Then Sir Henry tried, and failed.

Good took off a strong black handkerchief which he wore. He put it through the ring. 'Quatermain, take Sir Henry round his waist. Pull when I tell you to. Now!'

'Pull! Pull! It's moving!' said Sir Henry. Suddenly there was a breaking sound, then a movement of air, and we were all on our backs on the floor with a heavy stone on the top of us.

'Light a match, Quatermain,' Sir Henry said, when we had got up again. 'Carefully now.'

There, in front of us, were stone stairs.

'Now what should we do?' asked Good.

'Follow the stairs, of course, and hope for good luck.'

'Stop!' said Sir Henry. 'Quatermain, get the food and water. We may need them.'

I went back to our place by the boxes, and an idea came to me. I put my hand into the first box and filled the pockets of my coat. Then I put in a few of the big ones from the third box.

'Won't you take some diamonds with you?' I said to the others. 'I've filled my pockets.'

'Oh, forget the diamonds,' said Sir Henry. 'I hope I never see another one.'

Good did not answer. He was, I think, saying goodbye to the poor girl who had loved him so well.

'Come on, Quatermain,' said Sir Henry, already standing on the first step of the stone stairs. 'I will go first.'

'Be careful where you put your feet,' I answered. 'There may be some awful hole underneath.'

'There is probably another room,' said Sir Henry, as he went down slowly, counting the steps.

When he got to fifteen, he stopped. 'This is the bottom,' he said. 'There seems to be a path. Come down.'

We reached the bottom and lit one of the last two matches. We saw two narrow doorways, one to the left and one to the right. Which way should we go? Then Good remembered that the air blew the flame of the match to the left. 'Air blows in, not out,' he said. So we went to the right.

We walked slowly through the darkness for about a quarter of an hour. Then the path turned, or joined another path. We followed this, and in time we were led into a third path. And so it continued for some hours.

At last we stopped. We seemed to be lost in these endless

underground paths. We ate our last piece of meat and drank the rest of the water.

Then I thought that I heard a sound. I told the others to listen too. It was very faint, but it was a murmuring sound. No words can describe how good it was after all those hours of total silence.

'It is running water,' said Good.

We started again in the direction of the faint murmur, feeling our way along the rocky walls. As we went, the sound became clearer. We walked and walked until Good, who was leading, said that he could smell it.

'Go slowly, Good,' said Sir Henry. 'We must be close.'

Suddenly a cry came from Good. He had fallen in.

'Good! Good!' we shouted in terror. 'Where are you?'

Then an answer came back in a faint voice. 'I'm holding a rock. Strike a light and show me where you are.'

Quickly I lit the last match. Its faint light showed us a dark river running at our feet. In the river was the figure of our friend holding on to a rock.

'Be ready to catch me,' shouted Good. 'I'll have to swim.'

In another minute he caught Sir Henry's hand and we pulled him up out of the water.

'The stream is terribly fast,' he said. 'Only the rock saved my life.'

It was too dangerous to follow the river in the darkness. We had a good drink, and then went back the same way.

At last we came to a path that led to our right.

'We have nothing to lose,' said Sir Henry. 'All roads are the same here. Let's take this one.'

We were very tired and continued slowly. Sir Henry was now in front.

Suddenly he stopped, and we fell against his back.

'Look!' he whispered. 'Am I going mad or is that light?'

We gazed, and there, yes, far away in front of us there was a faint light.

With a cry of hope we continued. In five minutes there was no longer any doubt. A minute later a breath of real fresh air came to us. The path became narrower and Sir Henry went down on his knees. It became smaller and smaller. It was earth now. The rock had ended.

Sir Henry was out, and then Good, and then I was out too. And there above us were the beautiful stars, and the sweet air was on our faces. Then suddenly something fell away, and we were all falling through grass and small trees and soft wet earth.

I held a branch and stopped. A shout came from Sir Henry who had fallen to some flat ground. We found Good against a small tree.

We sat down together there on the grass and I think we cried with happiness. We had escaped from that terrible room where we had almost died.

The grey light of day crept down the side of the mountain, and we saw that we were at the bottom, or nearly at the bottom, of the deep mine in front of the entrance of the cave.

The day grew brighter. We could see each other now. Our faces were thin, our eyes were hollow, and we were covered with dust and earth and blood. We were a terrible sight. But Good's eyeglass was still fixed in his eye. Nothing could separate Good and his eyeglass.

We stood up and, with slow and painful movements, began to climb up the sides of the mine.

After more than an hour we stood on the great road. Beside it, about 300 feet away, a fire was burning in front of some huts, and round the fire were men. We moved towards them, supporting each other and stopping after every few steps. Then one of the men stood up, saw us, and fell on the ground in fear.

'Infadoos, Infadoos! It is your friends.'

Infadoos ran towards us, shouting, 'Oh, my lords, my lords, back from the dead!'

Chapter 14 Ignosi Says Goodbye

Ten days later we were back in our huts in Loo. We were not harmed too much by our terrible experience, but my hair was greyer and Good was never quite the same after Foulata's death.

We never again entered Solomon's treasure house. Two days after our escape, when we were feeling well again, we went back down into the mine. We hoped to find our way out of the mountain, but had no success. Rain had fallen and washed away our marks, and the sides of the mine were full of animals' holes. It was impossible to say which hole was ours.

We also returned to the great cave and even entered the Place of Death. We walked under Death's great spear and looked at the wall of rock. We thought of the old witch who lay underneath it. We thought of the beautiful girl who was dead on the other side. We also thought of the treasure. But although we examined the rock for an hour or more, we could find no sign of the secret way of opening it. Perhaps in the future a more fortunate man will discover a way in, but I doubt it. Millions of pounds of diamonds will stay in the three stone boxes until the end of time.

The next day we left for Loo. We were not too unhappy because remember, dear reader, I had filled the pockets of my coat with diamonds. Many of these were lost when we fell down the side of the mine, including most of the big ones. But many remained, including eighteen large stones.

When we arrived at Loo, we were welcomed by Ignosi. He listened with great interest to our wonderful story. When we told him about Gagool's end, he became thoughtful. 'That was a strange woman,' he said. 'I am glad that she is dead.'

'And now, Ignosi,' I said, 'we must say goodbye. You came with us as a servant, and now you are a great king. Tomorrow morning, will you give us some men to lead us across the mountains?'

Ignosi covered his face with his hands. Then at last he answered, 'I am very sad. Why do you want to leave me? You stood by me in battle and we won this peace together.'

I put my hand on his arm. 'Ignosi,' I said, 'when you travelled in Zululand, didn't your mother talk about this place? Wasn't your heart in your own land?'

'That is true.'

'In the same way, Ignosi, our hearts are in our land.'

There was a silence. Then Ignosi spoke again.

'I understand that your words are wise. Well, you must go. But listen, and tell the other white men my words. No other white man must cross the mountains. I will not see men who come to sell guns and strong drink. My people will fight with their spears and drink water, like their fathers. If a white man comes to my gates, I will send him back. If a hundred come, I will fight them. If an army comes, I will make war with all my strength, and they will not win. No man must ever come for the shining stones. But the path is always open for you three.

'My uncle Infadoos will guide you, with his men. I have learned that there is another way across the mountains. Goodbye, my brothers. Go now, before I cry like a woman. Goodbye for ever, my lords and friends.'

Ignosi stood and gazed at us for a few moments. Then he covered his face.

We went in silence.

◆

The next day we left Loo with our old friend Infadoos and his soldiers. As we travelled, Infadoos told us about a place to the north of Solomon's great road. There it was possible to cross the mountains and climb down their steep sides. He also told us that there was a kind of island of trees and rich land in the desert. We had always wondered how Ignosi's mother lived through the dangers of that long journey across the mountains and the desert with her child. It was now clear to us that she had gone that way.

At last we had to say goodbye to that true friend and fine old soldier, Infadoos. He, too, nearly cried. We shook his hand, his soldiers shouted '*Koom*!', and we began our climb down the mountain.

By the middle of the third day's journey across the desert, we could see the trees that Infadoos had spoken of. Soon we were walking on grass again and listening to the sound of running water.

Chapter 15 Found!

And now I must tell you about the strangest thing that happened to us in this strange adventure.

I was walking along quietly in front of the other two, when suddenly I stopped. There, sixty feet in front of me, was a little hut.

The door of the hut opened, and a white man dressed in animal skins came out. His right leg seemed to be broken, because he was walking painfully. He had a large black beard. I thought that I had gone mad. It was impossible. No hunter ever came to a place like this. Certainly no hunter would ever stay in it. I stood looking at the other man, and he stood and looked at me. At this moment, Sir Henry and Good came close.

Sir Henry looked, and Good looked, and then suddenly the man with the black beard cried out and began to come towards us. Then he fell to the ground.

Sir Henry ran to his side.

'George!' he cried. 'My brother!'

. . . suddenly the man with the black beard cried out and began to come towards us.

Hearing the sound, another figure ran from the hut. He too was dressed in skins, and he had a gun in his hand. When he saw me, he too cried out.

'Don't you know me?' he shouted. 'I am Jim, the hunter. We have been here for nearly two years.'

And he fell at my feet, crying with happiness.

The man with the black beard had managed to get up. He and Sir Henry shook hands again and again. They could not speak.

Sir Henry said at last, 'I thought you were dead. I have been over the Suliman Mountains to find you.'

'I tried to go over the Suliman Mountains nearly two years ago,' was the answer. 'But a rock fell on my leg and broke it. I have not been able to go forward or back.'

'How are you, Mr Neville?' I said. 'Do you remember me?'

'Isn't it Quatermain – and Good too?' he said. 'This is very strange, you fellows. You have made me a very happy man when I had given up hope.'

That evening around the camp-fire, George Curtis told us his story. He had heard from local people that this was the best way to the Suliman Mountains. They had suffered a lot while they crossed the desert. Then George had had his terrible accident, and they could not continue. Life in this hut seemed better than certain death in the desert.

'And so,' George Curtis ended, 'for nearly two years we have waited and hoped. But nobody has come to help us. I thought, brother, that you had forgotten about me long ago. And now you have left your comfortable life in England and you are here with me. It is the most wonderful thing that I have ever heard of!'

◆

Our journey across the desert was very difficult, especially as we had to support George Curtis. But six months later we were safe at my little house near Durban, where I am now writing.

◆

Just as I had written this last word, a postman came up the path with a letter. It was from Sir Henry Curtis:

1 October 1884

My dear Quatermain,

I sent you a letter a few weeks ago to say that the three of us, George, Good and I, reached England safely.

We went to London together. The next day Good was wearing beautiful new clothes, with a new eyeglass.

Good and I took the diamonds to Streeter's to discover their real value. I am afraid to tell you, because it seems such a huge amount. They advised us to sell a few at a time. We shall get a better price that way. They offered a hundred and eighty thousand pounds for just a few of the stones.

I want you to come home, dear old friend, especially as you want to give the third share to my brother George. You have done your life's work and have plenty of money now. There is a house quite close to here which will suit you very well. Please come. If you start immediately, you will be home by Christmas, and you must promise to stay with me for that.

Goodbye, old boy. I cannot say more, but I know that you will come. You know that it will make me happy.

Your friend,
Henry Curtis

Above my writing-table is the axe which I used to cut off Twala's head. I am sorry that we could not bring away the coats of chain armour.

HC

Today is Tuesday. There is a ship on Friday. I really think I must do what Curtis says. I will sail with her to England.

ACTIVITIES

Chapters 1–3

Before you read

1 Read the Introduction, then answer these questions.

a Which of these people or things appear in the story?
King Solomon   a witch   gold   love   a hunter   a writer
the British army

b What might modern readers like and dislike about this story?

2 Look at the Word List at the back of the book.

a Which are words for animals or insects?

b Which words are connected with fighting?

c Which words are for people?

While you read

3 Draw lines to match the people on the left with the correct description on the right.

a	Allan Quatermain	is a witch.
b	Sir Henry Curtis	has false teeth.
c	Captain John Good	is killed by an elephant.
d	Neville	died 300 years ago.
e	José Silvestre	has disappeared.
f	José da Silvestra	is a tall soldier.
g	Gagool	failed to find the diamonds.
h	Umbopa	is very rich.
i	Khiva	needs money.

After you read

4 Who or what are these? Why are they important in the story?

a the *Dunkeld*
b Bamangwato
c Inyati
d Sitanda's Kraal
e Sheba's Breasts
f the Kukuanas
g Ventvogel
h the Little Hand

5 Why do these people want to go to the Suliman Mountains?

a Quatermain
b Sir Henry Curtis
c Captain Good
d Umbopa

6 Discuss these questions with another student. What do you think?

a Quatermain says that the journey to the Suliman Mountains 'meant certain death.' Why? Make a list of the possible dangers. Which are the most serious?

b Why do Quatermain and the others travel the last 300 miles from Inyati to Sitanda's Kraal on foot? Is this a good idea? Why (not)?

c Look at a map of Africa. Find the Cape (Cape Town) and Durban. From Allan Quatermain's story, find the general area where Sitanda's Kraal might be. Which modern country is this in today?

Chapters 4–6

Before you read

7 Look at the picture on page 16. Imagine that you have to cross this desert on foot. In addition to water, write five more things that you will take with you. Compare your list with another student's. Which five things can you both agree on?

While you read

8 In which order do the adventurers do these? Number them 1–10.

a They eat uncooked meat. .....
b One of them kills a cow. .....
c They find water. .....
d They arrive at a large square. .....
e They meet Infadoos. .....
f They meet the king. .....
g One of them dies. .....
h They see a murder. .....
i They hear about Ignosi. .....
j They find a dead body. .....

After you read

9 Answer these questions.

Why:
a does Infadoos think that the adventurers are not human?
b does Twala tell Scragga to kill one of his soldiers?

What:
c is the relationship between Kafa and Twala?
d happened to Kafa's eldest son?

Where:
e does Quatermain tell Infadoos that he comes from?
f does Twala live?

Who:
g wants to look clean and tidy?
h says that many people will die soon?

10 Only two of these sentences are right. Which ones? Correct the others.

- **a** The adventurers find water in a cave.
- **b** The adventurers cannot sleep inside the cave because they feel frightened.
- **c** Ventvogel dies of thirst.
- **d** José da Silvestra drew his map with a bone and blood.
- **e** The adventurers do not cook the deer because they prefer cold meat.
- **f** The Kukuanas are afraid of Captain Good's eyeglass and clean shoes.
- **g** Infadoos's brother used to be king.
- **h** Infadoos's men are known as the Greys because of the colour of their eyes.
- **i** Twala has very cruel eyes.
- **j** Quatermain kills a cow.

11 Discuss these questions with another student? What do you think?

- **a** The Kukuanas do not understand Captain Good's false teeth and his eyeglass. They have also never seen a rifle before. What do you use in your country which people from other places might not understand?
- **b** What does Infadoos think of Twala? Why?
- **c** Why does Gagool want Umbopa to take off his cloth?

Chapters 7–9

Before you read

12 How will these be important in the next three chapters, do you think?

- **a** a snake
- **b** an eclipse of the moon
- **c** a dance
- **d** a battle

While you read

13 Are these sentences true (✓) or false (✗)?

a Umbopa's real name is Ignosi. .....

b Sir Henry and Captain Good are not interested in the diamonds. .....

c Gagool says that Umbopa is a bad man. .....

d The chiefs know that Umbopa is their real king because of the snake around his waist. .....

e The eclipse is Quatermain's idea. .....

f Captain Good saves a girl's life. .....

g Quatermain kills Scragga. .....

h Quatermain and Ignosi fight in the same group. .....

i The Greys attack Twala's army in Loo. .....

j Most of the Greys are killed in the battle. .....

After you read

14 Who is speaking? Who to? Who or what are they talking about?

a 'She killed my father with her words.'

b 'I will bring them here and show them that you are the real king.'

c 'Whoever harms him harms us.'

d 'If this man really is king, he must give us a sign.'

e 'It will begin at about ten o'clock tomorrow night.'

f 'She belongs to those stone figures.'

g 'Just wait and it will pass.'

h 'I do not expect to see tomorrow's sun.'

15 At the end of Chapter 9, how do these people feel? Why?

a Twala

b Foulata

c Ignosi

d Gagool

e Quatermain

16 Look at the map of the battle on page 36. Have this conversation between Twala and Gagool.

Student A: You are Twala. Describe what happened in the battle. You think you were unlucky to lose. Tell Gagool why.

Student B: You are Gagool. You do not think that Twala was unlucky. You think that he planned the battle badly. Tell him why.

Chapters 10–12

Before you read

17 What would you do now if you were

- **a** Quatermain?
- **b** Captain Good?
- **c** Sir Henry?
- **d** Ignosi?
- **e** Twala?
- **f** Foulata?
- **g** Gagool?
- **h** Infadoos?

While you read

18 Write the missing word.

- **a** Ignosi does not .... Twala because it is against Kukuana law.
- **b** Foulata looks after Captain Gold when he has a ....
- **c** It would not be possible for Captain Good and Foulata to be .... outside Kukuanaland.
- **d** Ignosi is not afraid of Gagool's ....
- **e** The bodies in the Place of Death have turned .... because of the salt.
- **f** Ignosi wears the .... that da Silvestra had taken from the secret room in the Place of Death.
- **g** Gagool kills ....
- **h** Gagool is killed under a ....

After you read

19 Work with another student. Have this conversation between Captain Good and Foulata in Chapter 10.

Student A: You are Captain Good. You want to take Foulata back to England with you. Tell her why.

Student B: You are Foulata. You want Captain Good to stay with you in Kukuanaland. Tell him why.

20 There are eight mistakes in this description of events at King Solomon's mine. What are they? Write the correct description.
Quatermain, Ignosi, Infadoos, Foulata, Sir Henry and Gagool arrived at the entrance of King Solomon's mine. They all went through a narrow door and walked along a wide path into a huge, brightly-lit cave filled with columns of ice. At the end of the cave, they went through a doorway into the Place of Death, where many dark figures sat around a large stone table. One of the figures was Twala, whose head was under his arm. Gagool moved a secret stone and they entered the treasure room. Foulata waited just outside the door.

Chapters 13–15

Before you read

21 How will the three men escape from the treasure room? Will they take the diamonds with them? Why (not)?

While you read

22 Circle the correct word.

a Sir Henry talks about *love/death*.

b Sir Henry and Captain Good *take/don't take* diamonds with them.

c At the bottom of the stone stairs they find *two doorways/a small river*.

d Outside the mine, the adventurers meet *Infadoos/Ignosi*.

e Two days after their escape, the adventurers return to the *Place of Death/treasure room*.

f Ignosi says that he will *fight/welcome* other white men in the future.
g Sir Henry's brother is living in a *cave/hut*.
h At the end of the story, Quatermain returns to *England/Kukuanaland*.

After you read

23 How do these help the adventurers to escape?
a a stone ring
b a black handkerchief
c the direction of the match flame
d a rock
e an underground river
f a faint light

24 Would Quatermain agree with these statements? Why (not)?
a Money is not important.
b Life in Africa is better than life in England.
c White men should stay away from Kukuanaland.

25 Which of these words describe Quatermain? Why (not)?
brave greedy cruel intelligent

Writing

26 You are Harry, Allan Quatermain's son. You hear about your father's plans to find King Solomon's diamonds. You are very worried about him, as a son and as a medical student. Write a letter to him.

27 You are Sir Henry Curtis. You want to go to Africa to find your brother. You want your friend, Captain Good, to come with you. Write him a letter. Explain why you need his help.

28 What happened to José Silvestre in the desert (Chapter 2)? Write his story.

29 Write José da Silvestra's story, from 300 years ago. How did he find the diamonds? Was he alone or was he with servants or friends? How did the witch cheat him? Why did he drop the bag of diamonds? Why did he die in the cave?

30 You are Quatermain. Your friend wants to find the diamonds. Write him a letter. Give him the details of how to find the treasure room. Warn him about the dangers.

31 Do you think that hunting animals for pleasure should be allowed? Why (not)? Write about the subject for a college magazine.

32 You work for a newspaper and you are sent to interview Sir Henry Curtis when he returns home. You know part of the story, but not the details. Write your questions and his answers.

33 You are George Curtis (Neville). Write about your time in Africa.

34 Imagine that you are Ignosi. Write a letter to Allan Quatermain five years after he has returned to England. What has happened in Kukuanaland during that time? What changes have you made? What has happened to Infadoos? Has anybody else tried to get King Solomon's diamonds?

35 Imagine that you and a group of friends try to get to King Solomon's diamonds in modern times. How does modern equipment make the job easier? How do you behave differently with the Kukuanas? What are your biggest problems? Write your story.

Answers for the Activities in this book are available from the Pearson English Readers website. A free Activity Worksheet is also available from the website. Activity worksheets are part of the Pearson English Readers Teacher Support Programme, which also includes Progress tests and Graded Reader Guidelines. For more information, please visit: www.pearsonenglishreaders.com

WORD LIST

armour (n) metal or leather clothing worn in the past by soldiers
axe (n) a metal tool with a wooden handle used for cutting wood
battle (n) a fight between two armies in one place
breast (n) one of the two soft, rounded parts on a woman's chest that can produce milk for her babies
cattle (n pl) cows
cave (n) a large natural hole in the side of a mountain or underground
chain (n) connected metal rings
column (n) something with a tall, narrow shape, made or formed of stone
creep (v) to move very carefully or quietly so nobody notices you
deer (n) a large wild animal that lives in forests and is killed for its meat
eclipse (n) a time when the sun or moon seems to disappear; there is an eclipse of the moon when the earth passes between the sun and the moon
elephant (n) a very large grey animal with big ears
feather (n) one of the light, soft things that covers a bird's body
fellow (n) an old-fashioned word for a man
forehead (n) the part of your head above your eyes
gaze (v) to look at someone or something for a long time
huge (adj) very big
mine (n) a deep hole in the ground from which gold, for example, is dug
murmur (n/v) a soft, quiet sound made by someone's voice
revolver (n) a type of small gun
rifle (n) a long gun that you shoot from your shoulder
shield (n) a large piece of leather or metal that people used to protect their body in a fight
snake (n) a long, thin animal without legs
spear (n) a long stick with a point at the end, used for fighting

stroke (n) a sudden hitting action; when you stroke something, you move your hand gently over it

thirst (n) the feeling that you need a drink urgently

treasure (n) a collection of valuable things like gold and silver

tsetse (n) an African fly that feeds on blood and can cause serious illnesses

wagon (n) a strong vehicle with four wheels, usually pulled by horses

witch (n) a woman who is believed to have magic powers; a **witch-doctor** uses magic to cure people